I0456990

THE BEE CREEK BLUES & MERIDIAN

AMERICAN CHAPTERS

GRETA GORSUCH

WAYZGOOSE PRESS

Book Design and Editing

Maggie Sokolik, Wayzgoose Press

Cover Design by DJ Rogers, Book Branders

CONTENTS

FROM THE AUTHOR

Welcome to our series, *American Chapters*. The *American Chapters* series presents short stories in vivid and easy-to-read 500-word chapters, perfect for English language learners internationally, and adult literacy learners in countries where English is commonly used.

All *American Chapters* print and ebook stories are also offered as audiobooks for learners who want to hear and read the stories and hear the sounds of American English.

American Chapters are lively, relevant, and realistic short stories about living in the United States of America. About Americans, immigrants, sojourners, and the diverse peoples living in this wide landscape, the stories touch on the tough questions, and the great things in life—things like work, ethnic differences, our connections to the past, our place in nature, being new, small town life, personal loss, and above all, new beginnings.

THE BEE CREEK BLUES

CHAPTER 1

IT'S TOO HOT!

The day was hot. The sun was bright. There wasn't any place to get cool. And it was only eight o'clock in the morning! Adrian Cooper looked at the shade under some short twisted trees with something like hope. He moved closer to the trees. At least he could look at them. He didn't know what they were called. They were not very tall. They were a sort of dark green. They were almost like pine trees, but they had dark blue berries under the branches. Adrian Cooper touched one. They were hard and dusty. These trees didn't look anything like the trees in Ohio. Ohio was where Adrian Cooper was from. Well, today, he was far from home.

"Cooper!" yelled Sergeant Hayes. "Get over here!"

Adrian sighed, and moved back into the strong, hot sunshine with the rest of the company. Tom Hart, Adrian's best friend, grinned at him. Tom offered Adrian a cup of water. Adrian drank it in about two seconds.

The men, about thirty of them, stood in an open field somewhere in Bosque (bos-KEE) County, Texas. They all looked hot and tired. They were covered in brown dust. They were in trucks all night to get to this place. The trucks were open, with just some hard seats and boxes. There was no way to lie down.

"Line up, and get some water," said Sergeant Hayes. The men lined up. Then Sergeant Hayes pointed down the hill. "There's a small creek down there. It's called Bee Creek. Bee Creek is the reason we're here. Get down there. You can wash up. Be back here in thirty minutes!"

Adrian didn't have to be told twice. He moved quickly with the men down to Bee Creek. The idea of cool water was wonderful. Getting all that dust off sounded great, too.

CHAPTER 2

SNAKE!

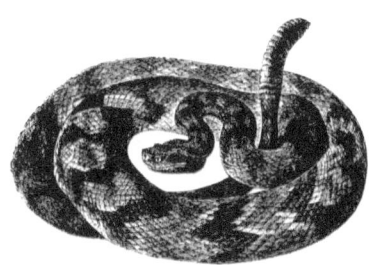

Bee Creek was small. There were lots of white rocks, and a few of the dark green trees with the blue berries on them. Then there was Bee Creek. Adrian could see only a thin ribbon of water. But the water was fast and cool. The men moved in a line along the creek bank to get to the water. Soon they were splashing each other. They got most of the dust off. One man, Riccardo Wilson, yelled, "Snake!" and the men went over to see. Just a few feet away was a brown, coiled snake. It was a rattlesnake. It rattled its tail, and backed up under some rocks. Riccardo Wilson picked up a large rock to kill it.

Adrian stopped him. "No," he said. "Let it be. This is his

creek. Besides, if we have to live here, that snake will eat the mice. You kill the snakes, up come the mice for our food."

Riccardo Wilson said, "Cooper, you think you're really something, don't you? You have all that school learning. Big college man from Ohio! You have ideas about everything. And now you want to save a rattlesnake?" He made "Ohio" sound like *ohhhhaaaaayooooo* and "ideas" sound like *ideeeeaaasss*. He shook his head. But he put the rock down.

Adrian felt a tap on his arm. Tom Hart grinned and said, "Aw, Riccardo just likes to talk big. Never mind him." Adrian laughed. It was true. Riccardo liked to talk and walk big. He was a big black man with a big chest and big hands. He talked like many African Americans from the southern U.S. Riccardo's words were all pushed together. At least that's what Adrian thought. But with a name like "Riccardo"... where did that come from? When Adrian Cooper asked Riccardo how he got his name, Riccardo just said, "My mama loved the opera."

"The opera?" asked Adrian.

"Yeah, the opera," said Riccardo. "Got any more questions, college boy?"

CHAPTER 3

SHOVELS

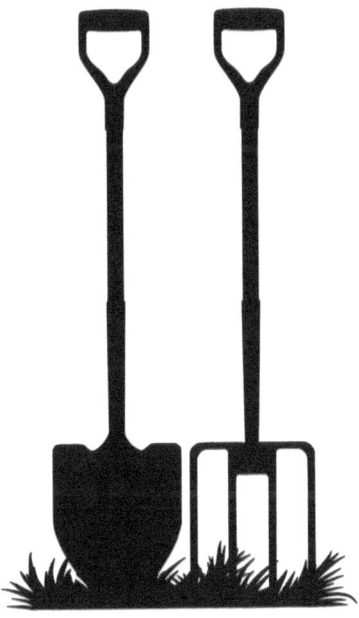

Sergeant Hayes yelled down the hill, "Breakfast! Get up here. Anyone who's not up here in five minutes goes hungry!" The men got up the hill. It was even hotter than before. Three more trucks were there. They were loaded with food, coils of rope, shovels, and small white tents. "Oh no," thought Adrian Cooper. The shovels were not a good sign. They had long wooden handles, and a sharp half circle of steel at the end of each handle. The shovels meant they would be digging dirt. He could work as hard as anyone else. But he hated shovels, and he hated digging dirt out in the sun.

The thirty men, and Sergeant Hayes, were the members of the CCC Company 1827. The "CCC" stood for "Civilian Conservation Corps." It was July 14, 1934. The United States was deep in the Great Depression. This meant that a lot of businesses closed. This meant that a lot of people didn't have jobs. This meant that a lot of people went hungry. This meant that a lot of people lost their homes. The CCC was started to make jobs for men who needed them.

The CCC was like the army. The U.S. Army ran the CCC but the CCC men like Adrian were not part of the U.S. Army. They were "civilians," which was the "civilian" part of CCC. The word "corps" in the army meant "a large group of men." That was the "Corps" part of the CCC. Each smaller group of men was called a "company." "Company" was also an army word. You did work for the CCC, and they fed you, gave you a place to live, and they paid you.

The CCC men did work in parks. They built park buildings, roads, swimming pools, and dams. They planted trees. This was the "Conservation" part of CCC. Anything that made a park better was called "conservation." The job of the CCC was to make parks great places to visit. They built small stone houses for park visitors to sleep in. Good roads were needed so park visitors could move around easily. And, dams were needed to collect water. Dams were built by hand at places with small rivers or creeks. Texas had few lakes, and there was not enough water in most parts of the state. Bee Creek, Bosque County, Texas, was a perfect place to build a dam. The dam would make a lake for fish. Visitors could go fishing. They could use the water for swimming. And the extra water could help the farmers in the area.

CHAPTER 4

OHIO

Adrian Cooper's CCC Company 1827 was at Meridian State Park in Bosque (bos-KEE) County, Texas. Their job was to build a dam across Bee Creek, and make a small lake. The men of CCC Company 1827 were mostly white, and seven were African American. Sergeant Hayes was black. This was unusual. Most CCC companies had white sergeants. But

Sergeant Hayes had been in the 1918 war in France. He had been a sergeant in the U.S. Army. That was easy to tell. He had the loudest voice any of them ever heard.

Adrian Cooper was 24. He was an African American man with medium dark skin and short hair. He had been a student at Central State University in Ohio. Ohio was far north of Texas. There were colleges with African American students in Ohio. But 1934 was a time when very few people, white or black, went to college. So, Adrian being in college was unusual. He was smart, though, and got a place at college. His mother and father worked hard to keep him there for the four-year course. Adrian's father was a farmer, a good one, but he died in an accident. His mother could not keep the farm by herself. M.J. Sims, a skinny black farmer who liked to talk, lived nearby. He wanted to use the farm. He could grow food to sell. It was good land. So, M.J. Simms took over the Cooper's farm. Adrian's mother moved to the city to be with her sister. Adrian had to leave college, where he studied life sciences. He wanted to be a teacher, more than anything. He joined the CCC. Maybe he could save money and go back to school.

CHAPTER 5

PEACHES

The men finished their breakfast of milk and warm bread. A small Mexican man came from town with large baskets of peaches on his horse and wagon. "Is for you and your men. Is *duranzos*... peaches," he told Sergeant Hayes in an accent. The men each got two peaches. *Duranzos* was Spanish for peaches.

They were small, but sweet. They were beautifully yellow, orange, and pink. The men ate them in about ten seconds.

"All right!" yelled Sergeant Hayes. "Fall in line!" The men fell in line under the hot sun. "All right, ladies," he began. Tom Hart laughed, quietly. Sergeant Hayes sometimes called them "ladies." No one knew why.

"You men over there!" Sergeant Hayes pointed to Adrian, Tom, Riccardo, and the four other African American CCC men. "Get the tents and rope off the trucks! You five over there!" he pointed to five of the white CCC men. "You do the same. Get the tents and ropes and put them over there." He pointed at a small hill with some of the short, dark green trees. The twelve men walked to the trucks. "Hey," said Adrian to one of the white men. He didn't know him. "Hey," said the man. He looked more like a boy. He was about eighteen. He was short but strong looking, and he had red hair. Together the men got the tents and ropes off the trucks and moved them over to the trees. It took two hours. By this time, the sun was too strong to work anymore. It was so hot, no one could even think.

Two more trucks with CCC workers came. The new men were covered in brown dust. They looked as hot as any person could be. The men of CCC Company 1827 ran forward with water. As the new men got off the trucks, each drank a large cup of water. Tom Hart handed a cup of water to a tall skinny white man with a large white hat. He said, "Thanks. Thought I was going to die of heat." Tom Hart smiled and said, "You're welcome."

"Hey," said the man. "Are you from Maryland? Maybe, eastern Maryland?"

"Yeah," said Tom Hart, surprised. "How did you know?"

"You sound like it. I can hear it. You have an accent," the

tall skinny man answered. "I'm from Royal Oak, Maryland. I'm Jonathan Roben."

Tom Hart grinned, showing all his teeth. "Ha! I can't believe it! I'm from Salisbury. That's real close to Royal Oak. I know that name, Roben. Lots of Robens around there."

"Yeah," said Jonathan. He looked around. "This is far from Maryland." Both men looked around at the hot, dry land. Jonathan asked, "What are we doing here?"

Adrian Cooper joined the two men. "We're building a dam across Bee Creek."

Jonathan was quiet for a minute. He sighed. Then he said, "I can't believe it. Is there really water around here?"

Both Tom and Adrian laughed. It was a question everyone asked.

There were two more sergeants, Sergeant Cobb and Sergeant Smithy. Both were older white men. They were turning red in the sun under their hats. They shook hands with Sergeant Hayes. Sergeant Cobb and Sergeant Hayes knew each other. They had been in the same war in France.

"All right men! Fall in line!" yelled Sergeant Smithy. He wasn't large, but he looked hard. "Fall in line! Move it!" He was almost as loud as Sergeant Hayes.

The men, now about sixty, fell into line. The sun was bright and hot. The sky was hard blue. No clouds.

"I'm Sergeant Smithy. We have a lot to do. So listen up! We have to get all the tents put up before lunch. No tents, no lunch. Got it?"

The men started talking at once.

"Did I say you could talk!?" yelled the Sergeant. "Shut up!" Now he *was* louder than Sergeant Hayes.

The men got quiet.

Sergeant Smithy continued, "The tents are to go up that hill. See those trees? See that flat place? That's where the tents are going."

CHAPTER 6

TENTS

Three hours later, the men of CCC Company 1827 put forty tents up. They used the coiled rope to pull up the thick white tents. There weren't many trees, but most of the tents were under some kind of tree. It kept some of the sun away. Each tent had two CCC men. Each of the sergeants got their own tent. The extra tents were for the engineers, cooks, and a nurse. The engineers were the ones who told the sergeants what they needed for the new dam. They would come in a few days. The engineers went from camp to camp. They only stayed a few days at each one. At one camp they were building a swimming pool. At another camp they were building roads.

While the men put the tents up, another truck came. There were three men, and a woman. The woman looked around the camp. She looked at the men working in the hot sun. The three men went to the back of the truck and pulled out big pots and pans and boxes. Then they started a cooking fire.

The woman, in a brown dress and hat, asked Sergeant Cobb where she could set up the nurse's tent. He showed her a spot. He called over two men from CCC Company 1827 to set up her tent. She said to Sergeant Cobb, "I don't like to see the men working in this hot sun. Are they getting enough water?"

Sergeant Cobb answered, "I'll make sure they get enough water."

The camp nurse nodded her head and went over to her tent. Sergeant Cobb and Sergeant Hayes brought a large barrel of water from a truck and put it near the men. Jonathan Roben and the young red-headed man ran to help.

"I guess you were pretty thirsty," said Sergeant Hayes to the young man.

"Yes I am!" said the young man. He drank a large cup of water. "I never saw it so hot."

The men of CCC Company 1827 could smell lunch cooking. They waited in line, and then Sergeant Smithy called Adrian, Riccardo, and Tom to help hand out food. Each of them had a big bag of bread. As the men went through the lunch line, they got bread, soup, another peach, and a cup of coffee. The men went to some rocks under the trees and sat down to eat. They were hungry. The cooks came around with more soup and bread. The nurse came out of her tent and got some lunch. She went back inside her tent to eat. After a few minutes, she brought out a medium-sized box to one of the cooks. Inside the box were cakes! There was enough for each man to have a small piece with more coffee. Riccardo Wilson looked happy. He had a sweet tooth.

That night it cooled off a little. The sun went down. The men sat in their tents and talked. The night was clear and dark. They could see thousands of stars.

CHAPTER 7
ROCKS

The next day, the engineers came. They went to look over the land where the dam would go. This dam would be harder to make than they thought. Bee Creek had some water, but not very much. There were a lot of large rocks where the dam needed to go. The rocks would have to be moved to one side, and broken up. Then the dam would be made of rocks and dirt. The men of CCC Company 1827 would have to do a lot of work. Breaking rocks, digging, and changing the shape of the land so it would hold a small lake.

"Are there other creeks or rivers here?" asked one of the engineers. He was young. "We need more water than Bee Creek."

Adrian Cooper was standing nearby. He walked over. He said, "I can walk around and look. I studied life sciences. If there's water, I'll find it."

"Where did you study?" said the engineer. Now another engineer, an older man, came over. The second engineer asked, "Are you the college boy? The one who went to Central State University?"

"Yeah, that's me," said Adrian.

The second engineer said to the younger engineer, "I heard about him when he first came." He looked back at Adrian, "How long do you need?"

Adrian answered, "Three or four hours. Less, if I can get help."

"Great," said the older engineer. "Take three or four men. Here's a map of the area. Write down where you find water."

Adrian went to Sergeant Hayes and got Riccardo, Tom, Jonathan, and Mackey, the young red-headed boy. Together with Sergeant Hayes they walked the land, looking for signs of water.

It wasn't so hot today. There were a few clouds in the sky. Mackey wondered if it might rain. "It feels like this in Kansas where I come from. Before it rains."

Adrian pointed to the north east where there were even more of the short, twisted trees. "I walked over there yesterday. I thought it felt cooler. I found a few snakes, too. They like water. Maybe there's a creek or spring." The men walked, and finally Sergeant Hayes said, "Over here!" The men came over. "Over here, too!" said Jonathan from another spot. Altogether, the men found four small springs. It wasn't a lot of water. But if you looked close at the rocks there, the rocks were wet with water. You could even see a little water coming up around the rocks.

Sergeant Hayes wrote "Little Springs" on the map. The men then walked west and crossed Bee Creek. It was a small creek, but the dark water moved fast between the rocks. The men looked at the map and walked west some more. Then Adrian called the men over. And there, at the bottom of a rocky hill was a large spring. Water came out from under some rocks and became a very small creek. It twisted and coiled in the direction of Bee Creek. The men followed the new creek on foot. In a few minutes they found where it met Bee Creek.

Sergeant Hayes marked the large spring on the map. He grinned and said, "This was good work today, men."

CHAPTER 8

WATER

Using the map showing the springs, the engineers made new plans for the dam. They could use the four little springs to the north east to add more water to the lake. But it meant more work for the men. The one large spring was too far away from the dam to use. But it might be used for something else.

"How long do you think the dam will take?" asked one engineer.

"Maybe three months?" said another. "Then another three months for the water to fill up. Then we have a lake."

That night, dark clouds came up. It rained hard. And the next night. The white tents were not much good in the rain. When Riccardo Wilson's tent fell down, he moved into Adrian and Tom's tent. He walked and talked big, and he slept big. He made a lot of noise, and no one got any sleep. Except Riccardo, of course.

The men started work the next day. Even with cooler weather, it was hard. The engineers left, and Sergeant Smithy was in charge. He had a map, and kept looking at it and shouting at the men. "You men there! Break up those rocks. Use those hammers!" Everyone hated rock breaking. They had to use large hammers. These were heavy long wooden things with a block of steel at the end. You lifted it high in the air. Then you brought it down on the rock as hard as you could. After ten minutes of that, it felt like your arms were coming off. In another ten minutes, your back started to hurt. Then your legs.

Four or five times a day the camp nurse came around with water. "Make sure these men drink enough water," she told Sergeant Cobb.

CHAPTER 9

FRUIT TREES

Sergeant Cobb took eight men for a special job. Adrian, Jonathan, and six others lined up. The Mexican "peach" man from the first day brought a large tent in his wagon. There were more large coiled ropes. Using the large tent and the ropes, Sergeant Cobb and the eight men worked to build a "community tent." It was large enough for all the men to sit and eat under. The small man stayed to watch. Then he left and came back with a wagon full of long tables and wooden chairs. The men set them up under the tent. Along with the tables and chairs, the Mexican man brought two large baskets of fruit. Adrian and Jonathan were taking a water break and saw the baskets. Jonathan took a cup of water and gave it to the Mexican man.

"Thank you, *gracias*," said the man. He smiled with all his teeth under a large hat.

"What are these?" asked Adrian Cooper. "These are peaches... what do you call them in Spanish?"

The man answered, "Is... *damascos*. Spanish for peaches."

"And these are... what? Apricots? What do you call them?" asked Adrian.

Before the Mexican could answer, the camp nurse came up. "Those are called *albaricoques* in Spanish."

Adrian and Jonathan were surprised. The nurse was just a normal American lady with light brown hair and blue eyes. She was middle aged, and spoke with a Texas accent. She said, "If you grow up in Texas, you learn Spanish." And she smiled at the Mexican man. "How are you Mr. Hernandez?" she asked. *"Cómo está?"*

"I'm good, is good," he said.

Adrian, who loved Mr. Hernandez's peaches, wanted to know something. "Where are you getting these peaches and apricots...uh, *albaricoques*?"

Paul Hernandez answered, "I grow them. I have land over there." And he pointed to the south. It was past where the dam would be.

Adrian asked, "You can grow this fruit here? Is there enough rain?"

Paul Hernandez said, "Oh, yes. I planted my trees five

years ago. If you know where to find water... *agua*... you can grow *duranzos y albaricoques*. You can grow many things. We do it in Mexico all the time. You have to find the right spot. With springs. Little water! Only a little. You don't need a lot of rain for these peaches."

"Cooper! Roben! Get over here! Finish putting up this tent!" yelled Sergeant Cobb. Adrian had an idea. He told Sergeant Cobb. Sergeant Cobb then went to Paul Hernandez and they talked. Mr. Hernandez agreed to return in December with fifty small fruit trees. Thirty would be peaches, and twenty would be apricots. He would show them where to plant the trees. When he saw the large spring west of where the dam would go he smiled. "Yes... yes. This will be a very good place for fruit trees." He said he would invite farmers he knew from Bosque County so they could help. They could learn how to plant and take care of young peach trees.

CHAPTER 10

BEES!

The work continued on the dam. July became August. August became September. September became October and then November. As the weather got cooler the work got a little easier. Breaking rocks, and moving large piles of dirt was still hard work. But at least the sun wasn't so strong. The dam started to look like a dam.

By November the dam was done. It was 600 feet long, and 40 feet high. It was made from concrete, rocks, and lots and lots of dirt. Concrete was a kind of man-made rock. It looked like a high wall that rose up and across the south end of the park. It was hard to believe that the men of CCC Company 1827 made such a big thing.

Soon after the dam was complete, the engineers closed the dam. This let water from Bee Creek and Little Springs to become a lake.

There were a lot of small difficulties. Tom Hart called them "the Bee Creek Blues." A few of the men hurt themselves while digging dirt or breaking rocks. The camp nurse took care of broken fingers and hurt backs. Men who were hurt got a few days off. Then, back to work. Two of the men thought that a rattle snake bit them. They yelled loudly. But the nurse checked their "bites" and found no snake bites.

"Did you put your hand on this?" she pointed at a small plant.

"Yeah… maybe," said one of the men.

"Well, that's a cactus," said the nurse. "If you put your hand on it, it will hurt you. Where are you from?"

The other man answered, "Illinois."

"You have roses in Illinois, don't you?" said the nurse. "Yeah, I guess," said the man.

"Well, these cactuses are just like roses. They have sharp spots. So don't touch them," said the nurse.

Riccardo Wilson, who had such a sweet tooth, got stung by bees one day. He saw a large group of bees over by the big spring west of the dam. He thought they might be in a tree, making a home. If that was true then there would be honey. It was months since he had anything sweet. He found an old tree in some rocks. He reached into a hole in the tree and…

"Ow!" Riccardo yelled. "Ow ow ow ow ow! Bees!"

He was so loud they could hear him all the way in camp. When the men brought him back to camp he had over fifty bee stings on his hands, arms, and face. The camp nurse pulled each stinger out.

CHAPTER 11

BORED

The camp nurse said to Sergeant Smithy, "Sergeant, the problem is that these men are bored. They only work. They don't have any time off. They need to go into town, meet other people."

Sergeant Smithy said something low and unclear. "What? What did you say?" asked the nurse.

"Yes, okay," said Sergeant Smithy. He could be loud when talking to the men, but not to the camp nurse.

"So," said the nurse, "This means the men can go into town tomorrow? And have half Saturdays off? And all Sundays off?"

"Ah," said Sergeant Smithy. "Well, the Saturdays and Sundays off are fine. But the people in town don't want the men to come."

"And why is that?" asked the nurse, sharply.

"Well, some of the men are black. That is a small town. Mostly white townspeople and farmers. They already don't like the CCC. Or anyway they don't understand the CCC. Some of the people in town have ideas that black men shouldn't be coming to town."

The nurse sighed. "So," she said, "that means that none of CCC Company 1827 can go to town, white or black?"

"Well," said Sergeant Smithy. "Yes." He looked unhappy about it. Then Sergeant Smithy called Sergeant Hayes and Sergeant Cobb over. They walked away and talked for an hour.

Then Sergeant Smithy and the nurse talked again. "We can take the men to Waco," said Sergeant Smithy. "It's an hour away. It's a bigger town. For the black men, Sergeant Hayes knows a black church they can visit on Sundays. The black families there can spend time with them. No shops are open on Sundays. But once a month we can go to Waco on Saturday afternoon. Then some of the men can do some shopping, stay overnight for church."

The nurse was quiet for awhile. Then she sighed. She said, "Alright. That's what we'll do."

So, for several months, the men of CCC Company 1827

went to Waco, Texas once or twice a month. They brought back books and newspapers and food. It helped a little with their boredom. A few times, some of the men went into the town close by. Jonathan Roben went, and do did Mackey. Both men brought back sweets and books. The sweets were for Riccardo. The books were for Adrian.

CHAPTER 12

A LETTER FROM HOME

The men waited for the water behind the dam to become a lake. It was very slow. But, bit by bit, more and more water stayed behind the dam. In a few more months it would look like a lake.

Adrian Cooper was bored. He missed being in college. He missed his books and his friends at Central State University. He still had a dream to be a life sciences teacher. One day he got a letter from his mother:

November 20, 1934
Dear Son,
It seems like such a long time since I saw you. I hope you're well.
Are you eating alright? Son, I have some news. Mr. M.J. Sims
came to my sister's yesterday.

The Cooper farm is doing well. Mr. Sims is making some money.
He plans to buy more land nearby.
Mr. Sims has asked me to be his wife. I think I will say "yes."

I know this will be a surprise to you. I loved your father. But
he's been gone for two years. I think about him every day. But I
also see a chance for a good life with M.J.

He asked about you. He remembers from when you were a boy.
He told me he could pay for you to go back to college. I think he
means it.

Please think on this. I will write again soon.

Love,
Your Mother, Ada Cooper

Adrian was surprised. He wasn't happy at this news. His mother and father always loved each other so much. He couldn't see his mother married to another man. And taking over the Cooper land! The land his father had worked on for so many years!

Feeling quite low and dark, he sat under a tree in the thin November sunshine. Tom Hart came over to ask if he was alright. Adrian handed the letter to Tom. After a few minutes,

Tom handed the letter back. They didn't say anything. Then Adrian said, "Of course I want to go back to college. I can't believe M.J. Sims is saying that. I don't know what to think." Tom didn't answer.

A week later, it was time for Thanksgiving. The cooks planned a big dinner with turkey. They even planned to have a special cake. The men of CCC Company 1827 missed their families. They should be eating Thanksgiving dinner at home.

Sergeant Hayes came back from Waco with a large box in the back of the truck. He and Sergeant Cobb carried the box into the community tent. No one could see what it was. After a few minutes the men heard music! Someone in Waco gave

Sergeant Hayes a phonograph! The men gathered around to listen to the records that came with the phonograph. They crowded close to hear music they knew, some jazz and some blues. But then they heard something they had never heard before. A *man* singing with a huge voice. It was opera! Most of the men had never heard opera before.

"Is that English?" asked one man.

Riccardo Wilson spoke up, "Nah, that's Italian!"

Finally, the cooks made the men leave. It was time to get ready for Thanksgiving dinner.

A few of the men went down to the water that was growing into a lake. Mackey said, "I'm leaving tomorrow."

"What?" asked Tom Hart. "Why?"

"I got a letter from my dad. He wants me to come back to Kansas," said Mackey. He looked very young. "I guess I want to go. I'm making money here. I get food. But I miss my family, too."

"I don't know," said Jonathan Roben. "I've been hearing about dust storms in Kansas and the states around there. How can you farm in a place where the land is just dust?"

Mackey shook his head. "Maybe the dust storms aren't as bad as they say," he said, finally.

Thanksgiving dinner was ready and all sixty men sat down to the best dinner they ever had. There was turkey, potatoes, tomatoes, bread, coffee, and finally peach cake. The men had never had peach cake before! The cooks made cake and then put the peaches on top with honey.

When the men sat drinking coffee after dinner, Sergeant Hayes got up and said that Riccardo Wilson had a surprise for them. The men looked at each other and started laughing and talking. "What's going on?" "Huh?" "I can't believe it." "Isn't he the one who got stung by bees?"

"Quiet!" yelled Riccardo, who stood up.

He walked to the front of the tent. He stood still. He waited. Sergeant Hayes started an opera on the phonograph. And then, Riccardo started to sing. And he could really sing! Riccardo could sing opera! He had a deep voice that the men could almost feel without hearing. He used his big chest and big hands to sing. He sounded just like the singer on the phonograph record. Truth be told, Riccardo sounded better than the singer on the phonograph. The song went on for minute upon minute. The phonograph ended. But Riccardo kept singing. And the men listened without making a sound.

When the song was over the men stood up and clapped their hands. They yelled and clapped their hands, and then that went on and on.

When it finally got quiet enough, Adrian said, "Where did you learn to sing like that?"

"I told you, my mama likes opera," said Riccardo. "She used to work in the opera house in Atlanta, Georgia. She was a cleaning lady. She took me with her, and I got to listen to opera." Riccardo grinned. "The singers in the opera company called me 'Riccardo.' Sounds Italian, I guess. Now, is there any of that peach and honey cake left? Or did you eat it all, college boy?"

CHAPTER 14

BUCKETS

Mackey left the next day. He picked up his bag of clothes, and climbed into a truck. Then he was gone. He was just a young boy, and very quiet. But his friends missed him.

In December, Paul Hernandez came to the Bee Creek dam with three wagons. There were fifty small peach and apricot trees, shovels, buckets, and some large bags. Some other farmers came to watch. Sergeant Cobb, Paul Hernandez, Adrian Cooper, a few farmers, and twenty other men of CCC Company 1827 worked all day to plant the trees. Some of the trees were put near the big spring west of the dam. Some of the trees were put closer to where the lake would be. For each tree, the men dug a hole with their shovels. They then put in some of the stuff from the large bags Paul Hernandez had brought. It smelled terrible. It was dirt and other terrible stuff from a pig farm in the area.

"Ugh!" said Tom Hart.

Adrian laughed. "It'll make those little trees grow."

After the men filled the dirt in around the trees, they went to the lake with buckets. They carried each bucket back, full of water. Each small tree got a large bucket of water.

"How often should we water the trees? For how long?" asked Adrian Cooper.

Paul Hernandez thought for a minute. He said, "Is best to water one time a week. One bucket of water. For maybe… three months? If it rains, you can stop watering for one week. In March, we should get rain…I hope! If there is no rain, keep watering."

Jonathan Roben asked, "Are you sure there's enough water here? I just can't believe it. It's so dry in Texas."

Adrian Cooper answered, "If they live for the first year, their roots will reach down for the water from the springs. Or from the lake. They might live."

Paul Hernandez grinned. Then he reached his hand out. Adrian and Paul shook hands. Then Paul Hernandez left to talk to the group of farmers who were standing nearby. He took his three wagons and left. A few farmers shook their heads. They didn't think the trees would live. But one or two more walked over to the trees. They looked at the land around the trees.

CHAPTER 15

THE LAKE

The following week, Adrian got another letter. It was from Central State University. It said:

December 10, 1934

Dear Mr. Cooper,
We wish to tell you that someone has already paid for you for one more year of school. We hope you will join us in January.

You can finish your college education. You need to be here by
January 12 if you plan to join us.

Sincerely, Wilfred Simpson
Head, Life Sciences Department

Adrian could not believe it. He had to sit down. His
mother was right. M.J. Sims meant to pay for Adrian to finish
college. It was his chance to be a teacher! He ran to Sergeant
Hayes and showed him the letter.

Sergeant Hayes said, "I think you ought to go. I wish I had
that chance. To go to college, to become a teacher. You will be
a great teacher."

Adrian decided then and there he would leave the CCC
and return to Central State University. He told his friends.
Tom Hart looked unhappy but said, "This is great for you."

Even Riccardo Wilson who didn't seem to like Adrian said,
"Back to college with you! Don't forget to tell everyone there
that you know a real opera singer!" Everyone laughed.

It was cold and windy on his last day. Adrian and Tom took
a last walk together around the park. They walked to the four
little springs. Then they walked west, around the new lake,
and found the large spring. Water still came up through the
rocks. Adrian put his hand into the cold, clear ribbon of water.
Adrian and Tom could see all the way down to the lake. There
were little fruit trees everywhere.

"This spring, those trees will look beautiful," said Adrian.
"I'm sorry I won't be here to see them."

"I'll make sure they get watered. Don't worry," said
Tom Hart.

They looked down at the Bee Creek dam. It held back a
lake that was almost full of water. Maybe in a few years, visi-

tors would come to fish, and sit beneath the peach and apricot trees.

Text message

April 14, 2017 10:20 AM

From Lacey Hernandez:

> *Maria, you have to come out here! I'm at Meridian State Park. You should see the amazing peach trees they have out here! The trees are covered in white flowers. Who knew?*

From Maria Wallace:

> *On my way! Where are you? Down by the lake?*

From Lacey Hernandez:

> *Yes. It's so beautiful here.*

MERIDIAN

CHAPTER 1

APRIL 1, 2017 THE MERIDIAN TRIBUNE, P. 13

The Meridian Tribune is looking for a reporter. We are looking for someone who can write about community news in our beautiful town. *The Meridian Tribune* is a small newspaper in Meridian, Bosque (bos-KEE) County, Texas. We have been a newspaper since 1893. We want a reporter who can talk to people, visit schools and homes, and report on important events. Photography ability is a plus. If interested, send a letter with writing and photography samples. Contact: Publisher Brett Mayfield, *The Meridian Tribune*, "Serving Beautiful Bosque County"

APRIL 3, 2017 THE MERIDIAN TRIBUNE, P. 7

We are happy to introduce our new reporter and photographer, Mr. Bill Wells. He is a recent graduate of the University of Texas. There, he studied writing and photography. He comes from New York, but lived in Texas for four years for university. He is looking forward to meeting the members of our town, and the small ranch and farm communities of Bosque County. Publisher Brett Mayfield, *The Meridian Tribune*, "Serving Beautiful Bosque County"

APRIL 3, 2017 THE MERIDIAN TRIBUNE, P. 14

For rent: Small three-room house, Meridian, Texas. This is an older home. It was built in 1896. It is in the center of town, and close to many shops and the county courthouse. Low rent. Pets OK. Perfect for someone new to the community. 145 Front Street, Meridian. Contact Miss Daisy Buchanan.

APRIL 7, 2017 THE MERIDIAN TRIBUNE, P. 1

Meridian Elementary and Junior High Schools to Close in May, by Bill Wells

The Meridian Elementary and Junior High schools will close in May, 2017. The decision was announced by the Education Department (ED). The ED says the two schools have too few students. Last September only nine new students started first grade, and only seven new students started seventh grade.

It costs too much to keep teachers at the school for each grade. The new ED lesson plans say that one teacher can teach only one grade. In other words, one teacher cannot teach first and second grades together.

"This is silly," says Mrs. Sonja Hernandez, a second-grade teacher at the school. "We have taught two grades together for many years. The older children can teach the younger children."

Mr. Mike Buchanan, the head teacher at the Meridian

Junior High School, agrees. "Our teachers do a great job. The students like working with different grades together. Our schools are important to the community. Our children grow up together, and their families come for basketball games and other community events."

The school closing plans show the problems that many small towns have. Meridian is a small farming and ranching community with only 1,400 people. Some young people stay in Meridian, but many don't wish to become farmers. After they finish high school they leave to find jobs outside Meridian.

It is not clear how the school closings will affect Meridian High School. From September, children at the elementary and junior high schools will be taken to school in Waco by school bus. The trip is over one hour long.

CHAPTER 2

APRIL 8, 2017, THE MERIDIAN TRIBUNE, P. 2

Wild Pigs Invade Bosque County, by Bill Wells

For the third time this week, Bosque County Sheriff's deputies were called to a ranch outside of Meridian due to trouble with wild pigs.

"We get large groups of wild pigs in spring every year," said Bosque County Sheriff Anna Morris. "This year is the same. You can get two or three mother pigs with lots of little baby pigs. They're hungry so they eat just about anything. You should keep your pets, your dogs, cats, inside at night. Wild pigs with babies will get into fights with family pets."

Miss Daisy Buchanan, owner of the ranch, telephoned the Bosque County Sheriff's office last night at 10 PM. She heard a lot of noise in front of her house. She went outside her home with her two dogs to check. A group of wild pigs was in front of her house. Miss Buchanan shouted at the pigs and they ran away. Two deputy sheriffs checked the area but the wild pigs were gone. They did, however, find a small brown dog in the dark. No one knows who the owner is.

"It's best to be careful. Don't leave any food out at night. Make sure you carry a light after dark," said Sheriff Morris. Anyone having trouble with wild pigs, or any other problems, should telephone the Bosque County Sheriff's office.

The small brown dog, "Cello," needs a home. Anyone interested in having a sweet dog should contact Miss Daisy Buchanan.

APRIL 14, 2017, THE MERIDIAN TRIBUNE, P. 3

Meridian High School Girls' Basketball Team Wins Over Albany, 86-84, by Bill Wells

The Meridian High School girls' basketball team won 86-84 over the Albany High School team. This was an exciting game. Both teams played well. Cassie Lopez, the tall star player for Meridian, held out against the team captain on the Albany team. More than 200 people attended the game.

After the game, the members of the two teams and their families had dinner together. The dinner was put on by the Future Ranchers of America, and included hamburgers and salad with iced tea. Then the Albany team returned home late by school bus.

CHAPTER 3

APRIL 30, 2017, THE MERIDIAN TRIBUNE, P. 2

My Walk Around Meridian, by Bill Wells

As you know I came to Meridian less than a month ago. Every evening after work, I walk around town with my little dog, Cello. Yes, I became the owner of that little dog. Miss Daisy Buchanan asked me to take him, and I did. Now my little house at 145 Front Street seems more like home.

On my evening walks, everyone says "hello." When I walk past the small supermarket, the owners ask me how I am. I tell them I'm fine. I ask them what kind of fruit they have today. They tell me they will have peaches in June.

Mrs. Bell at the drugstore next door tells me about her granddaughter, Miss Cassie Lopez, who will go to the University of Texas next year. She has a basketball scholarship.

As I walk past the Bosque County Courthouse, one of the sheriff's deputies says hello. He tells me the latest news. He tells me more about the wild pig problem out on the ranches and farms in the county.

We talk about the schools closing in May. He went to both the elementary and junior high schools. He asks me if I miss New York, and I tell him that walking around Meridian is a lot like walking around New York. People talk a little differently. Life seems a little slower. But there are lots of little shops, and I can walk everywhere, just like New York.

Finally, I stop at the Hernandez Ranch and Garden Center to look at the flowers and trees they have. I'm thinking about buying a small fruit tree to plant in front of my little house.

I want to thank everyone in Meridian. I feel very welcome here. Being a newspaper reporter here is exciting, and I learn something new every day.

Next week, look for an announcement about a photography contest to help keep open the Meridian Elementary and Junior High Schools.

MAY 10, 2017, THE MERIDIAN TRIBUNE, P. 3

Photography Contest to Help Keep Open Meridian Elementary and Junior High Schools, by Bill Wells

The University of Texas and the *New York Times* newspaper are having a photography contest. Everyone of all ages can send their photographs. The theme is "I Live in Meridian."

There will be first, second, and third prizes. For each prize, a donation of $1000 will be given to help keep Meridian Elementary and Junior High schools open. Our schools are very important for our community life.

The first prize winner will go to New York with Bill Wells. Each person can send up to two photographs for the contest. Send your photographs to Bill Wells by June 1, 2017 at the office of *The Meridian Tribune*, "Serving Beautiful Bosque County"

CHAPTER 4

MAY 17, 2017, THE MERIDIAN TRIBUNE, P. 7

Business Focus: The Hernandez Ranch and Garden Center, by Bill Wells

Each week we will focus on a different business in Meridian. We can understand this town better if we talk to the business owners. We can find out more about their stories.

This week we focus on the Hernandez Ranch and Garden Center. The Ranch and Garden Center is owned by Mrs. Sonja Hernandez and her husband Mr. Ruben Hernandez.

The business was started in 1910 by Ruben's great grandfather. Paul Hernandez came to Meridian to ranch in 1908, and he also had the first restaurant in Meridian. After a few years, he focused on his ranch and garden business, and in 1933 he started bringing fruit trees to the area.

Paul believed the weather in Meridian was good for peaches, apricots, and grapes. In fact, many ranches and farms in the area today have at least one tall, old peach or apricot tree planted by Paul Hernandez.

The Hernandez Ranch and Garden Center continues today. They have animal feed and tools for ranches and farms. They plant fruit trees for free. You buy the tree, and they help you plant it.

Everyone from Bosque County drives in to visit this business at least once a month. Mrs. Sonja Hernandez is also a second- grade teacher at the Meridian Elementary School. She sees many of her students and their families when they come to the center on Saturdays.

Hernandez Ranch and Garden Center is open six days a week. It is at 299 Front Street, just two blocks from the Bosque County Courthouse.

JUNE 10, 2017, THE MERIDIAN TRIBUNE, P. 2

Photography Contest Show at the Bosque County Courthouse, by Bill Wells

There will be a show for the "I Live in Meridian" photography contest this Friday night at 7 PM. Come to the Bosque County Courthouse and meet our three prize winners:

First place: Candy Fuentes, seventh grade, Meridian
Junior High School
Title of photograph: "Wild Pigs at Sunset"

Second place: Mark Schmidt, owner, Schmidt's German
Restaurant
Title of photograph: "Stone Wall with Peach Trees"

Third place: Daisy Buchanan, rancher and community
leader
Title of photograph: "Sheriff Anna Morris Rides

Her Horse"

The first place photograph shows Candy's three farm dogs looking at a group of wild pigs with the sunset behind them. The picture shows how the two different groups balance each other. The dogs need the pigs, and the pigs need the dogs, too.

Food will be served at the show, including fruit pies made from Hernandez peach and apricot trees across Bosque County.

Miss Candy Fuentes will be traveling to New York with her mother, Mrs. Albina Fuentes, and Bill Wells, reporter of *The Meridian Tribune*. They will meet the head of photography at *The New York Times*, and tour New York.

Candy will also have a chance to take some lessons on photography. "I'm so excited to go to New York!" said Candy.

$3000 was raised to help keep the Meridian Elementary School and Meridian Junior High School open in September.

CHAPTER 5

AUGUST 8, 2017, THE MERIDIAN TRIBUNE, P. 1

Reporter Hurt in Car Accident, by Brett Mayfield, Publisher

Two nights ago, Mr. Bill Wells was hurt in a car accident outside Meridian.

He was driving home after dark. He had gone to a meeting with ranchers about problems they are having with too little water and the rising price of animal feed.

While he was driving home, he turned the car suddenly. He went off the road into some trees.

Sheriff Anna Morris said, "It's possible he turned his car so he wouldn't hit a group of wild pigs. They come out after dark. His dog, Cello, was with him and was making a lot of noise. Luckily for Mr. Wells and Cello, someone heard the noise and telephoned us."

The sheriff and two deputies came out to help.

Mr. Well's injuries are light, and he is resting at home at 145 Front Street. He needs help with food, and taking care of his house and his dog. If you have some free time, please stop by and help him out.

Meridian Elementary and Junior High Schools to Stay Open, by Bill Wells

The Education Department (ED) said that the Meridian Elementary and Junior High Schools will stay open.

"With the extra money from the photography contest, we can keep the schools open," said ED director Kay Duke. "We are surprised at how many people telephoned us since May, and asked us to keep the schools open."

The ED also said that two grades could study together with one teacher. This will help save costs. And, older students can help younger students.

"It is great to see such interest in keeping our schools open," said community member Daisy Buchanan. "I went to the Meridian Elementary School when it had only two rooms. We have good schools today. The schools are so important to our community, and to our children."

I Live in Meridian, by Bill Wells

I want to thank everyone in Meridian, and beautiful Bosque County, for giving me a home. This is an interesting community. I can't imagine living anywhere else.

Each person has welcomed me. Everyone knows my name, and I know theirs. And, when I had a car accident, many of you stopped by with food. You helped me take care of my house and my dog. And now, I have three peach trees in my front yard, thanks to Mr. and Mrs. Hernandez.

I look forward to many years of peaches from those trees. I feel very lucky to be here. When my friends in New York ask me to return home, I tell them, "I live in Meridian. Beautiful Bosque County is my home."

Bosque County Courthouse

BOOKS IN THIS SERIES

American Chapters books by Greta Gorsuch

- *The Bee Creek Blues & Meridian*
- *Lights at Chickasaw Point & The Two Garcons*
- *Living at Trace*
- *Summer in Cimarron & Lunch at the Dixie Diner*
- *Cecilia's House*
- *The Storm*